THE RED BADGE OF COURAGE

The Young Collector's Illustrated Classics

THE RED BADGE OF COURAGE

By
Stephen Crane

Adapted by
Sara Thomson

Illustrated by
Jael,
Nick Block,
& Sean Gribbon

Cover art by Jael

Contents

Chapter 1
Going to War 11

Chapter 2
Henry's First Battle 27

Chapter 3
A Tough Fight 41

Chapter 4
The Wounded 55

Chapter 5
Henry's Red Badge 67

Chapter 6
Returning to Battle 83

Chapter 7
Following Orders 93

Chapter 8
Mule Drivers 107

Chapter 9
Crossing the Field 117

Chapter 10
   Carrying the Flag 131

Chapter 11
   Heroes 143

Chapter 12
   Sacrifices 157

Chapter 13
   Back to Camp 173

About the Author
   Stephen Crane 187

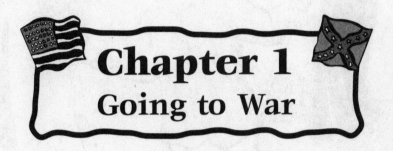

Chapter 1
Going to War

It was dawn of a new day in the Civil War, which raged between the Union and the rebel states in the America of the 1860s. Union troops, stretched out along the river banks, were coming awake. During the night, the camp fires of the enemy had gleamed like furious red eyes under the black brows of distant hills. Now that the night fog had lifted, the hills looked soft and green.

Waking up bright and early, a soldier went to the river to wash his shirt. There, he ran into a friend of his from the next camp who told him that the regiment would be sent to the front the next day. This friend had heard it from a cavalry man, who had heard it from a private, who had heard it from one of the orderlies at division headquarters.

The soldier ran back to his camp, waving his wet shirt on a stick like a banner.

"We're going to move tomorrow for sure," he shouted to the others. "We'll go up the river, cut across, and come around behind the enemy."

Bleary-eyed from sleep, their blue uniforms still unbuttoned, his fellow soldiers rushed out of their tents. When they had heard the news, they stood around and argued.

"It's a lie!" a soldier named Wilson said. He was short but had a thundering voice. "I don't believe we're ever going to move. We're stuck here. I've gotten ready to move eight times in the last two weeks, and here I am."

Jim Conklin, the soldier who had brought the news, felt that he had to defend himself. Nevertheless, he thought that he would be more convincing if he acted as if he were too sure of himself to need to produce proof.

"You can believe me or not, just as you like," he said.

Jim bustled about with self-importance while the rest of the soldiers argued with loud voices. Some took Jim Conklin's side, some Wilson's side.

Only one soldier kept to himself. His name was Henry Fleming. Henry was sick and tired of all this talk about marches and attacks. After a while, he went back to his tent and lay down on a bunk. So they were going to fight at last, he thought. Tomorrow there would be a battle, and he would be in it.

Henry had dreamed of battles all his life. In his imagination, he had seen himself as a hero—as the hero who would cast all former heroes into the shadow of his greatness. His young mind had been fired up by the stories of glorious battles he had read. The only thing that worried him was that present-day battles might not be as grand as battles in the past. He wanted to fight battles equal to those described in Homer's epic poems. Was that still possible?

Henry had burned to enlist. Tales of war were shaking the country: sieges, marches, and battles. There was glory to be gained, and Henry wanted his piece. His mother would have none of it, however. He'd be of better use staying on the farm, she had told him. She seemed to feel contempt for his patriotism.

Almost every day, the newspapers printed accounts of a great Union victory. Church bells rang in celebration of every piece of good news. People talked of nothing but the battles that had been won, and there was a thrilling sound of triumph in their voices. Henry had shivered with excitement as he listened.

One morning, he had woken before dawn. His mother was still asleep. He went into her room, leaned over her, and touched her on the shoulder.

"Ma, I'm going to enlist," he told her.

"Henry, don't you be a fool," she replied.

But Henry's mind had been made up. He went into town and enlisted.

The day he left for camp, Henry had embraced his mother tightly to wish her farewell and goodbye. He had imagined that, like a Spartan woman in his mythology books, his mother would tell him to return "with the shield—the symbol of your great courage—in your hand, or lying dead upon it." He had primed himself for a great scene.

"You watch out, Henry," his mother had said instead. "You take good care of

yourself. Don't go thinking you can beat the rebel army single-handedly, because you can't. You're just one little fellow amongst a whole lot of others. You've got to keep quiet and do what they tell you. Be a good boy. Don't you ever do anything that you wouldn't want me to know about."

Henry was disappointed, and angry at his mother for being so cautious. He could hardly wait for her to finish her speech, so he could leave.

He felt relief as he started walking away, but then he stopped by the garden gate and looked back. His mother was bent over the potato patch. Her back was quivering and tears were rolling down her face. Henry felt ashamed of himself.

This shame dampened his enthusiasm about the war as he walked on the road into town. However, when he got to town and his old schoolmates thronged around him with admiration, Henry swelled with pride, and his spirits soared once again. There was such a wide gulf, such a big difference, he thought, between the brave and noble who go to war and the meek and timid who choose to stay behind.

Henry joined the other young men from his town who had enlisted, and they all got on the train to Washington. He wore his bright new blue uniform

with pride. He looked handsome and dashing in it.

A crowd of townspeople came to see the soldiers off. To Henry it seemed as if all the young women were smiling at him with love in their eyes, and the old men looked at him with respect, as though he had grown in age and importance. People were treating him like a hero already, and he had not even fired a shot. Henry felt strong, invincible, ready for battle.

Once Henry had joined all the other soldiers who were encamped and waiting for orders to move into battle, his confidence began to weaken. Instead of the challenge and thrill of battle he had expected, there was nothing to do but stand around trying to keep warm. There were drills, of course, and reviews once a day, but even that grew to be monotonous.

With nothing else to occupy his mind, Henry thought about the war all the time. What if he were killed? What if he were wounded? What would it be like to charge ahead, while bullets were coming at him? Did he have it in him not to run from gunfire?

Henry had never doubted himself before, but then, he had never been put to the test before. He started to worry that he might run. Just the thought of it made him panic and shudder with shame. The long, boring months that he had spent in camp thus far were like unending torture.

Now, at last, thanks to the news he had overheard this morning, the time had come. The next day, his regiment would move to the front—into the line of fire.

Henry got up from his bunk and went outside. Wilson and Jim Conklin were still arguing.

"Oh, you'll see fighting this time, all right!" Jim Conklin said.

"I don't believe it," said Wilson. "Just rumors."

"Didn't the cavalry start out this morning? Everyone has been saying that there's hardly any cavalry left in camp," Jim Conklin said.

Wilson had nothing to say to that.

"Ready for tomorrow, Henry?" Jim Conklin asked as Henry joined the conversation.

Henry looked away. "Think any of the men will run?" he wondered out loud.

"Oh, there may be a few of them who'll run, especially when they first go under fire," Jim replied.

"Did you ever think that you might run yourself?" Henry asked him.

"If a whole lot of men started to run," said Jim, "I suppose I'd start to run. But if everybody was standing and fighting, I'd stand and fight like a demon. You can bet on it."

"Huh!" said Wilson, who was a bit older than Henry and Jim. "There's many a man who thought he was going to do great things before the fight, but when the time came, he took to his heels."

"That may be true, but I'm not going to take to my heels," said Jim. "The man who bets on my running will lose his money."

Henry walked away from them. He had felt relief when Jim Conklin admitted

that he would run if others did. But when he said that he'd stand and fight if everyone else stood and fought, Henry's feeling of relief had vanished.

Henry walked to the riverbank and lay down on the grass. The blades pressed tenderly against the nape of his neck, and the soft breeze felt like a caress on his face. The early-morning light was

clear and bright, but the hilltops were
still covered with the pink haze of sun-
rise. Normally, he would be milking the
cows on the farm at this time.

Henry remembered how angry he used
to get at having to get up this early. He
would kick at the milking stools, rattle
the pails, and curse the cows! Now, he'd
give everything he had to be back at the

farm. He was a farmer, whether he liked it or not. He was not made to be a soldier. Whatever had made him think that he was?

The buzz of excited voices of the other soldiers carried over from the camp. Henry was too far away to understand what was being said, but the sound went through his ears like a fearful shiver. These other soldiers were made to be soldiers, he thought. They held together as a group because they were alike. He had never felt so completely alone—so completely different from everybody around him.

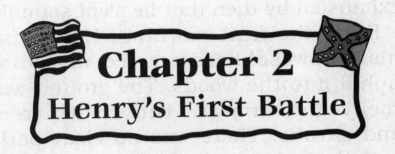

Chapter 2
Henry's First Battle

The next morning, Henry's regiment was given its orders. The troops went across the river and marched the whole day. Henry imagined that the enemy was hiding in the heavily wooded hills that surrounded the valley. He marched in great fear. The enemy would come at them like a wild animal leaping from its cave, he thought. They might attack at any moment. Would Henry stand and fight? Would he run?

Nothing happened that day, however. At night, the troops were ordered to camp at the foot of a hill. Henry was so exhausted by then that he slept soundly.

Early the next morning, Henry and his fellow soldiers started marching uphill into the woods. The ground was rocky and uneven, thick with trees and shrubs. There was no clear path, and the soldiers had to break ranks. By noon, they were all grunting and

sweating. Most of the soldiers had taken off their shirts and had gotten rid of their knapsacks, so they would not be weighed down. They looked tired and beaten.

Henry wanted to lie down and rest for a while, but he was afraid that the men coming after him would trample his body. It was like being trapped in a rushing mob—he was being carried forward without a will of his own. Even if he wanted to, he could not escape. He did not feel like a soldier going to battle but like an animal in a herd being driven to slaughter.

At last, they got to the top of the hill. Looking down the other side, Henry could see small battles being fought. Amidst the brown and green of the trees, he could see the blue and gray of the soldiers' uniforms and, now and then, a red flag. There was a spattering sound of gunfire, and the loud boom of explosions.

So, this was it! A battle!

This hillside looked to Henry like the wrong place for a battlefield. Henry had imagined that the two armies would be coming head to head. In this situation, however, the enemy could come at them from anywhere. Enemy soldiers were scattered all around the forest. Just a moment ago, Henry had stepped over the body of one of them. The dead soldier was lying on his back, with his eyes open. The wind was making his beard rise and fall. It looked as though an invisible hand was stroking it. Henry felt a chill run up his spine.

"The generals don't know what they're doing," he thought. "They are leading us into a trap. We'll be killed like pigs." He could not believe that he was the only one who realized this. "I have to tell the other soldiers," he thought. "We have to do something." But when he looked at the other men, he saw that there was no fear or doubt on their faces. He was

afraid that if he spoke up, they would think he was a coward and jeer at him.

Henry kept silent and did what everyone else around him was doing: He built a mound out of dirt, sticks and stones and hid behind it. He had barely completed his small fort, when the regiment was ordered to abandon its position and move farther down. Here, too, the men

built small, makeshift forts only to be told to move again. This went on and on.

Henry lost patience. "I can't stand this any longer," he cried. "I don't see what good it does to make us start and stop for nothing. I didn't come here to walk around and dig holes."

The soldier next to him opened his mess kit and took a hearty bite out of a sandwich. "Shut up, you little fool!" he said to Henry.

Henry could not understand how this man could eat at a time like this. His own stomach was in knots. The time spent waiting was killing him. For all his fear, he wished that the battle would start. He wanted to get it over with. Better death than the anxiety of not knowing if he could pass the test of manhood—if he would be proven brave, or run.

Other regiments, farther down the slope, were engaged in battle. There was so much smoke blowing uphill, it was hard to see what was going on. The sound of explosions and gunfire seemed to be approaching, however, as the fighting men moved uphill. It was like listening to the roar of an oncoming train.

Suddenly, soldiers came running out of the smoky haze. Behind them and all around, shells started exploding. Bullets whistled among the tree leaves, nipping off small twigs. More and more men came running toward Henry. Following at their heels was the enemy, advancing like a furious swarm, yelling and firing their guns.

The brigade's first attack had been fought off unsuccessfully. Now, it was up to Henry's regiment to hold back the enemy.

The captain of his company paced to and fro among his men. "Reserve your fire!" he shouted at them. "Don't shoot until I tell you! Wait till they get really close!"

The gunfire was getting heavier; the smoke was getting thicker; the sound of explosions seemed a constant, deafening din.

Henry wiped the sweat off his face with his sleeve. Had he loaded his gun? What if he had not loaded his gun?

When the enemy was in plain sight at last, he did not stop to think whether he had loaded his rifle or not. He fired a first, wild shot. He did not worry if he was aiming right; he did not worry if he might get shot. He just pulled the trigger. He kept firing and reloading his gun with furious haste.

He no longer felt like one person. It was as though the danger of death had united him and his comrades into one body and one soul, and he was fighting to save that larger body, not his own. He went at it as if he were doing a job: fire, reload; fire, reload. As far as he could see, everyone else was fighting the way he was. No one was striking heroic poses. They loaded their rifles, jerked them onto their shoulders, and fired into the billowing smoke.

Gradually, the return fire began to dwindle. Henry realized that his side was winning. As the smoke thinned, he could see that the enemy had scattered.

"We've held them back! We've held them back!" the men cried.

Henry's eyes hurt and were tearing from the smoke. His throat was parched,

but he wanted to laugh with joy. He took a sip of water from his canteen and looked around him. Dead soldiers lay scattered in every direction. Their arms were twisted, their heads bent, their bodies contorted as though they had been dumped onto the ground from high up in the sky.

When his thirst was satisfied, Henry realized that the artillery fire had not altogether stopped. A din, like distant thunder, came up from both sides of the hill. He looked around again. To the left and right, deeper in the forest, he could see more lines of troops marching into battle. Here and there, raised up high and waving in the wind, were red-striped flags. In the smoke-filled air, they looked like birds flying fearlessly through a storm.

Chapter 3
A Tough Fight

The next morning, Henry woke with a feeling of tremendous joy. He had passed the test! He had proven to himself that he was not a coward. He had fought like everyone else, and then some! He was a fine, brave fellow.

For the first time, Henry felt close to his comrades in his brigade. He chatted and kidded around with them. They had fought together; they had faced death together. He loved every single one of them. Everyone seemed to feel just the same as he did. Everyone had a big grin on his face.

Then, all of a sudden, the men heard the distant thudding of marching feet. They turned toward the field and could see a mass of enemy soldiers steadily approaching. They looked to be thousands strong.

A cry went through the camp like an uproar: "Here they come again! Here they come again!"

The men became solemn. They were exhausted from the fighting of the day before. Their muscles were stiff and their bones ached as they walked to their ranks.

"We're never going to withstand this second attack!" the soldier next to Henry said. "What do they expect us to do—fight the whole enemy army all by ourselves?"

Henry was so tired, he felt weak at the knees. How could the enemy have the

strength to march, to launch a new attack? This had to be a mistake, he thought. He kept staring at the enemy soldiers, as though he expected them to stop, make a bow of apology, and turn away. They couldn't possibly have the strength to fight.

The soldiers in Henry's brigade had no time to get their bearings. Artillery shells began exploding all around them. The enemy infantry was coming at them from the front, and enemy gunners from the left and right. The smoke was becoming thick, and was spreading like a black cloud.

All Henry could see near the front line were red flashes of gunfire. He kept firing his gun furiously, as he had the day before. This time, however, the men who were positioned ahead of him started to run from enemy fire. They ran, howling with fright. Almost immediately, the men along his line threw down their guns and ran as well.

Henry panicked. He, too, threw down his gun and fled. There was no shame on his face. He ran through the smoke like a blind man. He wanted to run to the rear, but he did not know which way the rear was. He kept stumbling into trees and falling down. He was terrified. It seemed as if he were being hit from all directions.

How much easier it would be to bear death, he thought, if one were hit between the eyes. One would see it coming, at

least. It would be dreadful to be hit between the shoulder blades, and not know it was coming. He tried to run faster, so that the men running behind him would get hit in the back first. The closer he got to the front of the pack of fleeing soldiers, the safer he would be. Everyone seemed to have the same thought. It was like running a race.

Just as Henry managed to get up front and lead the way, a shell came swirling over his head and exploded at his side. He hurled himself to the ground and rolled into some bushes. By the time he got back on his feet, the rest of the men were ahead of him. He did not want to be last, and be the first one hit with gunfire, so he decided to take off on his own. He went in another direction, through some thick shrubbery and bushes. This way, it would be easy to hide if the enemy came upon him.

After just a few steps, to his amazement, Henry came to a clearing where a

Union battery battalion was stationed. At ease and as jovial as could be, fellow soldiers manning the Union cannons were shooting at the enemy battery across the field. "It was easy enough to keep your cool when the enemy was so far away," Henry thought. He would like to see how relaxed and smiling they would be if the enemy infantry came at them, and they had to fight face-to-face. He felt contempt for these men who felt so safe behind the big guns.

Henry walked past the gunners, to an area where he could see an army camp. The troops were in formation, standing still. A general, seated on a horse, was listening to a cavalry officer, who seemed to be communicating some information

to him. Clearly, it was the wrong information. The general's face was beaming.

Henry hurried over. He should be the one talking to the general, he thought. He knew what had happened. He knew that unless the general gave the command for the troops to retreat, they would be slaughtered.

As he drew closer, he could hear the general saying, "They've held them back! We'll wallop them!"

Could it be that his regiment had won, after all? Could it be that only a few men from his company had fled, while the rest had held their positions?

From far off, Henry could hear cheering. It was his regiment! The men must have won!

Henry felt both amazed and angry. Until that moment, he had believed that he had not been a coward, that it had been right that he had run away in order to save his life. He was a small piece of the army and, in saving himself, he reasoned, he had saved a small piece of the army. Of what use to the army would he have been if he had died? Alive, he could fight again. He had done the right thing. The wise thing.

He felt bitter about his comrades who had stood their ground. They were ignorant fools. They lacked foresight. They should have all fled, at least until reinforcements came. That was the way to win a battle. Nevertheless, he was afraid to go back to his regiment. His comrades were too stupid to understand his point of view. He was sure that they would make fun of him if he went back.

Henry felt great self-pity, that he should be so misunderstood. He felt despair. He walked along with slumped shoulders and a bowed head. He wanted to put off the moment of being reunited with his comrades as long as possible.

Instead of going straight back to his encampment, Henry decided to walk around in the forest. He walked and walked until he could no longer hear the cheers of the soldiers.

The sun blazed among the leaves, and the dappled light looked like the soft light inside a church. Birds chirped and flew lightheartedly from branch to branch. A butterfly swooped over a clump of weeds, fluttering its soft wings. Everything was beautiful and peaceful. It was as if Nature knew nothing of the roar of war. It was as if Nature had no ears.

Henry felt better. He noticed a squirrel on the ground, nibbling an acorn. Henry

picked up a pinecone off the ground and threw it playfully at the squirrel. The squirrel scurried away. "See that!" he thought. "The squirrel recognized danger and fled. The squirrel did not stand its ground and try to fight." It was Nature's way to flee from danger. Nature was of the same mind as Henry.

He walked on with a lighter step. He felt good about himself. Just as he was beginning to relax, however, he sensed

that someone was staring at him. Henry was terrified. There was a dead man right in front of him, sitting up, with his back resting against the trunk of a tree. The bright blue color of his uniform had faded to a dull brown. His mouth was gaping, and his lips looked gray. His eyes were wide open and dull like the eyes of a dead fish. All over the ashen skin of his face ran hundreds of black ants.

Henry gave a horrified shriek. He was too frightened to move. When, at last, he was able to move his legs again, he walked backward, keeping his eyes on the corpse. He was afraid that if he turned his back, the dead soldier would spring to his feet and come after him.

When he felt that he was at a safe distance, Henry turned around and ran as fast as he could. The ground under his feet was swarming with black ants. They were following him, he thought. They were coming after him. He held on to a tree and listened carefully. He imagined he could hear a menacing growl coming out of the dead soldier's throat.

Chapter 4
The Wounded

Henry's experiences in the forest after running from battle had lasted a long time. It was late evening now. The slanting rays of the sun bathed the forest in a reddish-bronze light, like the reflection from a far-off fire. Henry had sat down to rest a while against a tree. Suddenly, there was a tremendous roar—the ripping sound of bullets, the thunderous boom of artillery shelling, and many savage war cries. It was as if the earth was being torn apart. The two armies were battling again. From the enormousness of the sound, it seemed to be a full-fledged battle, not the small skirmishes that had been going on all day.

Henry listened quietly for a while, then started to run in the direction of the battle. He wanted to go to the edge of the forest, so he could peer out. He wanted to watch.

As he neared an open field, he saw that the ground was littered with corpses. He hurried across, walking over and around the dead men, until he reached a clearing. From there, he could see the battlefield at some distance. Hundreds of wounded soldiers were streaming out of the field in a steady flow. The men hobbled along, forming a long procession.

Henry decided to join them. When he caught up, he walked next to a soldier who had been shot in the head and in his right arm. His head wound was bound with a blood-soaked rag. His

wounded arm dangled from his shoulder like a broken tree branch. His uniform was tattered, and his body and spirit looked tattered, as well.

"It was a pretty good fight, wasn't it?" he said timidly to Henry.

Henry pretended not to have heard, and walked faster.

The tattered man kept after him.

"The boys were mighty brave, weren't they?" he said. "Not a single one of them ran."

Again, Henry hastened his pace, but the tattered man would not leave him alone.

"Where were you hit?" he asked.

Henry broke into a run and slid away into the crowd. Here, too—everywhere around him—everyone was wounded. Henry felt ashamed that he was not bleeding. He looked at the wounded men with envy. He wished that he, too, had a wound—a red badge of courage.

He walked as fast as he could, but men in the lines called out to him to slow down, so as not to make his wounds worse. Henry slowed down so that they wouldn't suspect the truth.

Just ahead of him walked a tall soldier who was groaning with pain. Something about him seemed familiar. Could it be? Henry thought, amazed. Yes, it was Jim Conklin!

Henry ran up to him.

"Oh, Jim! Oh, Jim!" he cried.

"Hello, Henry."

Jim held out his hand for Henry to

shake. It was mangled, gory with blood and torn flesh. Henry could not bring himself to touch it.

"I've been worrying about you, Henry," Jim said. "I thought you might have gotten yourself killed."

"Oh, Jim!" Henry said. He put his arm around his wounded friend's shoulders and tried to support him.

"You know what I'm afraid of, Henry?" Jim said. "I'm afraid that if I become too

weak and fall down, the artillery wagons will run me over."

"I'll take care of you, Jim," Henry said. "I swear to God."

"Just pull me out of the road if I fall down. That's all I ask," Jim said.

Henry tried to keep his sobs from bursting from his chest. He walked by Jim's side silently for a while. Suddenly, he felt a hand on his shoulder.

It was the tattered man.

"You'd better take your friend into that field," he said. "There's a battery coming. It will run him over if he can't move any faster."

"Come on," Henry coaxed Jim. "Let's move to the side."

Jim Conklin straightened himself, pushed Henry away, and walked toward the field. He started to run.

"Jim! Stop! You'll hurt yourself!"

"Get away from me!" Jim said. "Don't touch me!"

He rushed toward a wooded field.

Then he stopped and stood motionless. From the calm expression on his face it was clear that he had reached the place he had been looking for. He seemed to be waiting for someone whom he had come there to meet. Suddenly his chest swelled, and Jim gave out a roaring groan. He collapsed on the ground, falling straight down like a felled tree. His mouth gaped, as if he were grinning.

Henry ran to his friend and knelt by

his body. Jim's jacket had flapped open
in the fall, and Henry could see his bare
chest. It looked as if Jim had been
chewed to pieces by wolves.

"He had courage," the tattered man
said. "He died like a real hero."

Henry threw himself on the ground
and wept, sobbing like a child.

"We've got to get going," the tattered
man said. "Your friend's up and gone.
He's left us. There's nothing we can do

for him now. We have to look out for ourselves."

Henry got up. He saw that the tattered man looked ashen in the face. He was staggering, as though he had no more strength in his legs.

"Good God!" he cried. "Not you, too!"

"Never say die," the tattered man said.

They walked on in silence.

"You look pretty bad yourself," the tattered man said to Henry after a while. "You must be hurt real bad. Where is your wound? It must be bleeding inside. Those are the worst kind, wounds that bleed inside. You die before you know it. Where does it hurt?"

"Oh, don't bother me," Henry said.

He was furious. It was as if the tattered man was raising a flag of shame that waved, for all to notice, from the flagpole of his curiosity.

"Don't bother me!" Henry said again, walking faster.

"You'll do yourself harm, walking fast

like that," warned the tattered man. "You shouldn't walk fast with a bad wound."

Instead of replying, Henry climbed over a fence and ran along on the other side. When he was at a safe distance, he turned around. The tattered man was wandering helplessly in the large, empty field.

Chapter 5
Henry's Red Badge

From his place near the fence, Henry became aware that the roar of the battle he had set out to observe was getting louder. He could not see the battlefield from where he was, so he went around the small hill that was blocking his view. Now he could see that many of the troops were retreating. The road was thick with wagons, cavalry, and infantrymen. Henry was comforted by this sight.

Perhaps he was not so bad, after all. Hundreds of other men were retreating.

Then he saw a fresh column of infantry heading toward the din of battle. They were crisscrossing the retreating troops. There was eagerness and strength to their step, despite the fact that they were marching through a section of the army that was retreating in defeat.

Henry was stunned. The men were

walking tall, confident, and proud, as though their weapons were made of fire and their flags of sunlight. They looked superhuman.

Henry wished that he could be like them. He would give his life to be able to be like them. In his imagination, he saw himself dust-stained, haggard, panting, flying to the front line and throttling the enemy with his bare hands. Oh, how he wished he could die heroically before everyone's eyes! He quivered with the desire to be in the midst of such proud, courageous men.

It wasn't too late. He would go to battle with them! He would run and join the advancing column!

How could he? He couldn't fight with just any regiment. He would have to find his own. It would be a miracle if he could find his regiment in this commotion, and even if he did, how could he face his comrades? They would be able to see it written on his face that he had fled earlier. They would look at him as if he were a worm.

Even if he could brave the humiliation that would surely come at the hands of his fellow soldiers, Henry did not have the physical strength to fight again. He was weak from hunger and had a scorching thirst. His face was so dry and dirty he thought he could feel his skin crackle. Every bone in his body hurt. His feet were like two sores. When he tried to walk, his head wobbled from exhaustion.

He just wasn't like those brave soldiers. He did not have the makings of a hero. Realizing this caused him to feel self-hatred and despair. Henry started wishing that the advancing regiment would be defeated by the enemy. The courageous men he envied would scurry away like chickens and become just like him. He could then say that he had run just a little bit earlier. It would prove that he was more intelligent than they.

He had sensed what was coming and had acted with foresight.

If the Union won, on the other hand, it would confirm for everyone that Henry had run out of fear. He would never be able to live down his dishonor.

To ease his conscience, Henry said to himself that he did not wish the army to lose the war; just this one battle. He was sure that the Union would win in the end. What would it matter to lose one little battle? From the bottom of his heart, he wished that the army would lose, just this once.

A moment later, however, he was horrified that he had wished such a thing. How could he even have such thoughts? He was worse than a villain, he thought. He was totally contemptible. The army should win gloriously, and he should face the humiliation he deserved.

He imagined the whole regiment saying, "Where's Henry Fleming? He ran, didn't he? Oh, my!" They would question him with sneers and laugh at his stammering explanations. "There he goes!" they would say with scorn, each time he walked by.

Yes, he thought. He deserved all the ridicule in the world.

Just as Henry was beginning to accept his fate, he saw dark waves of men coming out of the woods. They were the men he had seen advance with such heroic

courage. His wish had come true. They were stampeding like terrified cattle. Oh, no! he thought. Oh, no!

Henry was devastated. The men were running in a frenzy. He ran downhill and tried to speak comforting words to them. He wanted to show them that he understood how they felt, but they kept shoving him out of their way. They did not care to hear what he had to say. One man pushed him so hard that Henry fell down on his face and hit his head on a rock.

Henry lay on the trampled grass, too weak and dazed to get up. He was afraid he would be crushed. All around, he could hear the thudding of running feet and the clatter of hooves and wheels. From a distance came the constant grumble of cannons. Close by, the gunfire sounded like pounding hail. Shots were coming from all directions.

At last, Henry felt able to struggle up onto his hands and knees. With great effort, he pushed himself upright. His

head hurt. He touched his forehead, and the pain made him scream out. When he looked at his fingers, he saw that they were covered with blood.

The fleeing men had gone around the hill. There was no one left on the road. Here and there lay overturned supply wagons. Henry had to weave his way around them. He had to walk slowly, because the wound on his head hurt. He was so tired, he wished he could just lie down on the road and sleep.

After a while, he could see small bonfires burning in the distance. It had to be the camp! If his feet could carry him that far, he would find shelter at last. He had to keep walking, no matter how hard and painful it was.

When he drew closer to the camp, he could see several men standing around the fires. In the red light and surrounding darkness, they looked like menacing ghosts. Strewn over the ground were bodies of men, curled up

under blankets. Henry thought that they might be dead, and was horrified. No, they were asleep. He was sure that he could hear them snore.

"Halt! Halt!" A figure came out of the darkness, pointing a rifle at him.

"Why, it's you, isn't it, Wilson?" Henry stammered.

"Henry? Henry Fleming? That you?"

"Yes, it's me."

"Am I glad to see you!" Wilson said. "I thought you were dead."

Henry could barely stand on his feet, but he tried to pull himself together. He had to come up with a lie fast. He had to explain his desertion.

"I've had an awful time of it," Henry said. "I got separated from the regiment and ended up way over yonder, to the right. There was terrible fighting. I got shot in the head. You've never seen such fighting! I got shot, like I said."

"Got shot!" Wilson cried with concern. "Why didn't you say so right away?"

"Who are you talking to, Wilson?" another voice asked. "Henry, is that you? Where were you?"

It was the corporal.

"I got separated ..." Henry began.

"He's been shot," Wilson interrupted. "We must get him some help."

The corporal inspected Henry's wound. "This looks bad. You must be in great pain," he said.

"Yes, it hurts. It hurts awfully bad," Henry said.

"Come, we'll take care of you," said the corporal gently.

They led Henry close to the fire, and dressed his wound.

"Here you are," said the corporal. "Just as I thought. You've been grazed by a shell. You did a great job on the field today, Henry. You made us proud. Now, get some rest."

Wilson cradled Henry's head tenderly in his arms and gave him some hot coffee out of his canteen.

"You look awful right now," Wilson said, "but I bet that you'll feel much better in the morning."

Wilson brought over his blanket, and laid it over Henry's body.

"Go to sleep now," he said. "You need to sleep."

"I can't take your blanket," Henry said.

"You need it more than I do," Wilson said. "You got shot. You nearly got yourself killed."

"How are you going to sleep?"

"Don't you worry about me," Wilson said. "You need to rest."

Henry said nothing. A deep drowsiness came over him, and he closed his eyes. Off in the distance, he could still hear artillery fire. Did the enemy ever sleep? he thought. He was too tired to answer his own question, or even to care. He drifted off into a deep, dreamless sleep.

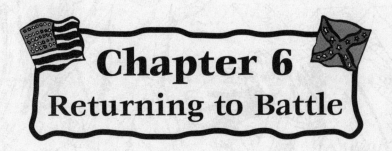

Chapter 6
Returning to Battle

When Henry woke in the morning, he felt as if he had been sleeping a thousand years. Yet the war was still raging. The sound of artillery and cannon fire had increased, and seemed to be closer. In the dim dawn light, the faces of the sleeping soldiers in his regiment looked gray. The men lay motionless, and at first Henry thought that he was surrounded by corpses. He gave a shriek of horror and sat up.

Now, he could see that a few other men had awakened and were stretching their limbs. The bugle sounded reveille to wake everyone up. From deep in the woods came the thunderous sound of a

drumroll. Grumbling and swearing, the sleepy men rose to their feet.

"How are you feeling, Henry?" Wilson asked.

"Pretty bad."

Henry's head felt as if it had swollen to the size of a melon.

"Let me look at your wound," Wilson said.

As he tried to change Henry's bandage, Henry screamed at him.

"Go easy! Go easy, I tell you! You are the clumsiest man I know. You're all thumbs. I'd rather have someone drive nails into my head than have you change my bandages."

"Come now, come now," Wilson said softly. "I'm almost done."

When he was finished, he patted Henry on the back.

"Come eat," he said. "Food will make you feel better."

Wilson skewered some fresh meat on a stick, roasted it over the fire, and gave it all to Henry. For himself, he poured some strange-looking, mud-colored mixture from a tin pail. Wilson watched Henry wolf down his food, happy that his friend had a hearty appetite.

Henry was amazed at Wilson's kind-

ness. Wilson used to be a braggart—full of himself and selfish. He used to strut and try to look tough. Now, his face had softened and his eyes looked as if they had aged. He seemed unsure of himself.

"You've changed," Henry said.

Wilson looked ill at ease. "It's true," he answered.

"Oh," Henry said casually. "Jim Conklin is dead."

"Jim Conklin! Dead?" Wilson looked as

if he were about to cry. He was really shaken up.

"Well, Henry," he said anxiously. "What do you think our chances are? Think we can win?"

"Why, Wilson! The day before yesterday, you would have bet you could lick the enemy all by yourself," Henry said.

Wilson lowered his eyes. "Perhaps, I would have," he said. "I was a big fool."

He pretended to stoke the fire, so that

Henry would not see the shame on his face. After a while, he said in an uncertain voice: "The officers say we've got the enemy boxed in. We've got them just where we want them."

"Oh, I don't know about that," said Henry. "From what I've seen, it's the other way around. We got a real pounding yesterday."

"I thought we handled them pretty well yesterday," Wilson said.

"What do you know!" Henry said. "You saw nothing of the fight."

"About half the regiment came back wounded. Just like you," Wilson said quietly. "They had been scattered all over, fighting with other regiments. Just like you."

Was there irony, and a hidden sneer, in Wilson's voice? Henry was angry. He now believed his own lie—that he had fought and had been shot. It was only right that he be treated like a hero.

"What are you trying to say?" he said angrily.

But Wilson looked at him sadly and said nothing.

Still, Henry was ready to pick a fight. He would have, too, if the corporal had not come around that moment.

"To your ranks!" the corporal yelled. "On the double!"

Henry and Wilson took their positions in the formation. Henry's wound still hurt, but he was in great spirits. After his terrible ordeal yesterday, his confidence in himself had grown. He was now a man of experience. Like the hero in a fairy tale, he had come face to face with the dragon. He had escaped death.

Henry remembered some of the men he had seen the day before, men who had run from battle. Their faces had been terror-stricken, and they had run like scared mice. He, at least, had fled with dignity. In any case, no one knew he had fled. In the eyes of his comrades, he was a hero. He could keep his head up.

He recalled the battle scenes he had observed, and imagined how he could talk about them when he got home. The people from his hometown would listen with their mouths open. They would drink up every word, and imagine him at the center of each blazing battle. The young women would swoon at his feet, and the older men would treat him with respect and awe.

Looking over at Wilson, Henry felt superior to him. Poor Wilson had had the wind knocked out of him. He had a worried, meek expression. He was scared. But Henry was not scared. Henry was no longer afraid of anything.

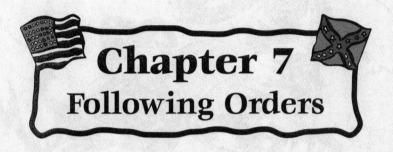

Chapter 7
Following Orders

Henry's regiment had been given new orders: The men were to march deeper into the forest and dig lines of trenches. The troops huddled behind the small embankments they had made, and waited for their turn to fight. By the look and sound of things, the battle would not start for a while. The din of cannon blasts and gunfire was coming from a great distance.

Wilson, who had not gotten enough

sleep the night before, buried his face in his arms and dozed off. Henry was on the lookout for the enemy's approach. The trees were in the way, however, so he could see only a small part of the battlefield. It was not an encouraging sight. The troops who had been fighting through the night were still carrying on, but their return fire was sporadic. The flags that had been planted over their trenches drooped pitifully, as though already in defeat.

To the left and right, several more battles

were going on. As on the day before, the sound of gunfire was coming from all directions. Soon the enemy started moving closer to where Henry and his fellow soldiers were waiting. The sound of battle became deafening.

Once again, the men in Henry's regiment were being surrounded as the battle raged closer. The enemy was closing in, strong and confident that they would win. Their cries of triumph were tearing up the air.

Orders came for Henry's regiment to abandon their trenches and move forward into battle. It was as though their own generals, the generals of the Union Army, were deliberately leading them into a trap. What chance did they have, with the enemy coming at them from three sides?

"Our commanding officers are idiots!" Henry shouted with rage.

"You said it, brother!" a soldier next to him replied.

Henry cursed his commanders with every step he took.

Wilson walked next to him, with stooped shoulders and a bowed head, like a man who has taken a beating.

"Maybe it's not the general's fault," he said meekly. "He's doing the best he can."

"Oh, yeah?" Henry said. "Whose fault is it then? We fought like heroes yesterday. We did our part!"

He did not believe he had said that! The lie shamed him at first. However, when he looked around him and saw that no one questioned his words, his shame vanished.

"No other regiment fought the way we did," he said. "No one can say we did not fight like heroes."

It made him feel brave to repeat this lie. It gave him courage.

"No one can say that," Wilson agreed.

"Well, then!" Henry said. "It can't be our fault that we lost. It has to be the general's. I don't see the use in fighting my heart out, just to be whipped because the general doesn't know what he's doing."

A soldier, who was walking ahead of him, turned his head and looked at Henry sarcastically.

"You talk like you fought the whole battle by yourself, Fleming," he said.

Henry blushed.

"Why, no ..." he stammered. "I didn't mean that."

"Oh, no?" the man said.

Henry was cut to the quick. The sarcasm of the man took all the wind out of his sails.

The troops had come to a small clearing. From the woods around them came a crackling sound, as though the trees were on fire. The sun had risen in the sky, and the light was clear and bright. The air was calm. No leaf or blade of grass was stirring. It was like being in the eye of a storm.

Suddenly, there was a loud explosion of shells. It sounded like rolling thunder. The men stood motionless, in shock.

Henry felt a violent hatred for the enemy. He was not going to stand there and take it. He was not going to be cornered like a rat. He crouched behind a tree and aimed his rifle.

"They're not going to chase us, by God!" he said. "They had better watch out."

"If they chase us, they'll chase us into the river," Wilson said. "There's nowhere for us to run."

"They're not going to chase us," Henry shouted.

His fingers tightened furiously around his rifle. He not only hated the enemy soldiers, he despised them. They had chased him and his comrades this way and that, like boys do when they chase a helpless cat. Now, they had them where they wanted them—in this tight spot by the river. Well! Henry was going to show them that he was no helpless kitten. Henry was going to fight back!

He ran forward, shooting his gun wildly. He could not see well in the smoke. More than once, his feet got caught in the underbrush of the forest and he fell. He worried that he might have been shot, but he did not care. He got back up on his feet and continued firing his gun.

The barrel of Henry's rifle had become so hot from constant use that it burned the palms of his hands. It was as if he were holding hot coals. Gun smoke choked his throat and hurt his eyes.

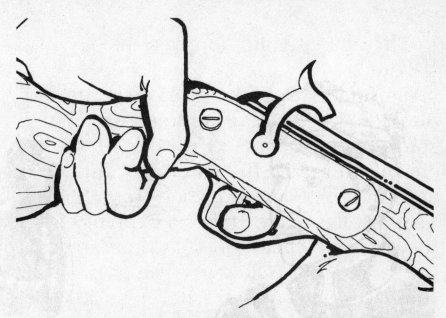

His skin chafed from the gunpowder in the air, and his face was filthy with soot. The blood from his head wound had dried, making the bandage stick painfully to his raw skin.

Henry did not pay much attention to any of these things. He was barely aware of his discomfort and pain. He fought like a dog that keeps fighting, mindless of its wounds. He just could not stop.

A deep silence had grown all around him, but he kept firing his gun.

"Don't you know when to quit?" a

hoarse voice behind him said. "There's nothing to shoot at!"

Henry turned around and looked in the direction of the voice. His comrades, in row after row behind him, were staring at him with wide-eyed astonishment.

Henry turned his head again and looked ahead of him. The ground was

deserted—the enemy had been routed. All that was left was a cloud of smoke.

"Oh!" he said. He took a swig of water out of his canteen to soothe his parched throat.

"If I had ten thousand men like you, Fleming, I could win the war in one week," said the lieutenant of his company.

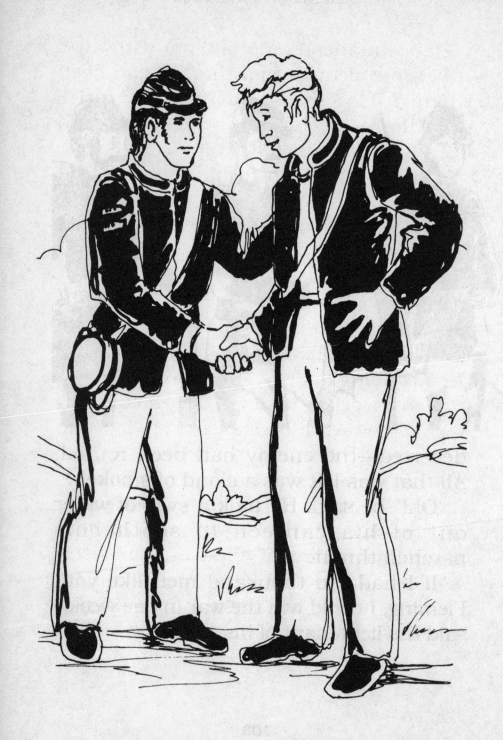

His comrades stared at him with awe. It became clear to him that he had been firing furiously at nothing for quite a while, and that his comrades had been watching.

Wilson walked up to him and nudged his arm.

"Are you all right, Henry?" he asked him. "Are you all right?"

"Yes," Henry said quietly.

He was still stunned. He had fought like a hero, and it had come to him quite naturally! He had not even been aware he was doing it.

"Good work, Fleming!" the lieutenant said. "Good work on the part of all of the men in this regiment!"

It pleased Henry to hear the praise, and to see the admiration in the eyes of his comrades. Still, he could not fathom how it had all come about. It had been so easy!

Before, when his bravery had been a lie, Henry had carried on and on about how brave he had been. He had boasted, because he wanted to cover up the shame of his cowardice. The more he boasted, the less others would be able to see through to his lie, he had thought.

Now that his bravery was real, he was silent. He felt humble.

Chapter 8
Mule Drivers

The soldiers in Henry's regiment barely had time to catch their breath and rejoice, when it became clear that the enemy was preparing a new assault. The trees seemed to quiver from the boom of explosions, and the ground seemed to shake from the pounding feet of the advancing army. The smoke had cleared, briefly, but it soon became thick again. It was as if a black fog were drifting in from the forest.

A horrible scream tore through the air.
One of the men had been hit by a shell.
He fell on the ground, twisting in agony.

"I'm dying," he cried. "Water, water.
Please give me some water."

There was no more water. Everyone's
canteen was empty.

"Let's go fetch some water from the
stream," Wilson said to Henry.

"What stream?" asked Henry. He had
not seen any stream.

Wilson felt certain that they had passed a stream on their way to the battlefield. He went back to look for it.

Henry went along, thinking "If Wilson is right, and we find the stream, I'm going to drink gallons and gallons of water. I'm going to throw myself in and soak my body."

They wandered about, but they could not find the stream. While they were searching, they reached a part of the forest that was on high ground. From here, they could see a large field down below. It was swarming with retreating troops. Wounded men hobbled along, while others lay exhausted on the ground.

In the midst of this crowd, they could see cavalry officers riding high on their horses. One man was sitting majestically on his horse and made no movement at all. Henry and Wilson recognized him at once: He was the general of their division.

One after another, officers galloped their horses up to the general, saluted him, and listened solemnly, while he gave them orders.

"Let's walk up close and hear what they're saying," Henry said.

They mingled with the troops and walked as close to the general as they could without being discovered.

"The enemy is getting ready for another charge," the general was saying. "It will be directed against Waterside, and I'm afraid they'll break through our lines there, unless we stop them first."

The officer to whom he was talking was trying to keep steady on his rearing horse. He was unsteady on the saddle and could barely bring his arm to his cap to salute.

"It will be mighty hard to stop them," the officer said.

"I imagine so," said the general.

He began to talk rapidly in a low voice. Wilson and Henry could not make out his words. Then, in a loud, impatient voice he said :

"What troops can you spare?"

"I can't really spare any, sir," the officer said. "There's only the 304th regiment, and they are a sorry bunch of men. They fight like mule drivers."

Henry and Wilson were appalled. The 304th was their regiment.

"They'll have to do," said the general. "Get them ready. They'll have to attack in five minutes."

The officer saluted, turned his horse around, and galloped away.

"I don't believe any of your mule drivers will make it back," the general shouted after him.

The officer shouted something back in reply and smiled.

Henry and Wilson hurried back to their comrades.

A sorry lot! Mule drivers! Henry felt as if he had aged years just in the last few minutes. It was as if he were seeing the war and the army with new eyes. The general wanted to sweep the danger away, so he thought he could sacrifice any old regiment to do the job. They might as well be brooms.

When he and Wilson got back, the lieutenant was furious at them.

"How long does it take to get water?" he yelled. "Where have you been?"

His angry expression changed to alarm once he had taken a closer look at them. Henry and Wilson were so scared,

their eyes were wide open, and the blood had drained from their faces.

"We're going to charge!" they said. "We're going to charge!"

"Charge?" said the lieutenant. "Charge! Well, by God! Finally, there'll be real fighting."

The soldiers who were standing nearby started asking questions.

"Are you sure?"

"Charge! What for? What at?"

"Henry, are you telling the truth?"

"Cross my heart and hope to die," said Henry.

"He isn't lying," said Wilson. "We both heard the general give the order."

"How could you hear them talking?" asked a soldier, who still refused to believe them.

"We were right there," Wilson said.

The soldier nodded thoughtfully and went back to his post.

A moment later, officers started bustling about, giving orders for the troops to get into close formation. They yelled at any soldier who did not move fast enough. They looked like anxious shepherds trying to herd their sheep into a pen.

All around, the air was torn with the sounds of war. In the far distance, the smoke was so thick that it looked like storm clouds. Straight ahead, it was impossible to see beyond the thick foliage of the trees. The enemy was hidden in the dark shadows of the forest. There could be thousands of them lying in wait.

Henry shot a secret glance at Wilson, and Wilson returned his look. They were the only ones who knew the truth. Their general believed that they were not going to make it back. He was sending them to their deaths, and he could not care less.

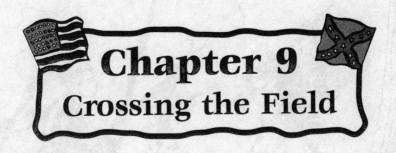

Chapter 9
Crossing the Field

From the corner of his eye, Henry spotted a young officer who looked like a mere boy. He was galloping on his horse and waving his hat. His gesture represented the command to advance. The soldiers in Henry's regiment were packed so closely together, they moved forward like a single furious beast. Henry was jostled on his feet and pushed forward. He was not moving by his own will. He was being pushed and

shoved, as if by a rushing mob. He had
to struggle to find some space for himself so he could move his arms and
legs freely.

He ran toward the forest as fast as he
could. He could not see, but he could
feel the danger that lay behind the
trees. He wanted to come face to face
with it. He wanted to get it over with. If
he had time to think, he knew that he
would become frightened.

As he drew closer, red flashes of gunfire lit up the shadows among the leaves. It looked like the trees were on fire.

Until then, the troops had been moving in perfect formation. As soon as they entered the woods, however, the men scattered among the trees. Suddenly, it was as if each man were fighting on his own behalf.

Henry kept up his mad pace. Shells

were exploding all around him—on the ground, over his head. The sound was deafening, and the smoke was clouding his vision. To Henry's right and left, men were falling, dead or wounded.

At last, the troops came out of the woods and into a small clearing. Henry could see the enemy's battery and, just ahead, the enemy's infantry line. It looked like a gray wall surrounded by a cloud of smoke. The regiment rushed at it with a thundering yell.

The battle went on, in fits and starts. The troops would go on the assault and attack the enemy line, then stop to let the smoke clear, and then they would go on the assault again. Whenever they stopped, exhaustion and anxiety came over them, and their faces looked tense and worn. But when they rushed the enemy again, their strength and courage came back and their faces shone with courage.

It was as though, suddenly, every

single man had become fearless and unselfish. No one seemed to care about risking his life. They seemed to be mindless of the danger they faced.

Henry felt just as fearless and unselfish as his comrades. It was wonderful to experience such unselfishness and courage. It was sublime. It did not matter why the war was being fought. The only thing that mattered was the regiment. Henry was fighting for his comrades. He was fighting to save their lives. He wanted to die for them.

It was marvelous to experience such love.

He looked around him. Many soldiers were shot dead, and many more lay wounded on the ground. With every new advance, the number of troops who went forward dwindled.

It was a terrible sight to see. The shrieks of pain and the desperate moans of the dying were paralyzing. The remaining soldiers went on moving and

fighting as though dazed. After a while, they slackened their pace.

"Come on, you fools!" the lieutenant screamed at them. "You can't stay here! Come on!"

He marched ahead, waving them forward with his arm, but the men did not follow.

The lieutenant turned around.

"Come on, you rascals!" he cried. "Come on, you stupid mules!"

The insults roused the men. They leapt forward like maddened leopards. Henry was the first to lurch forward. He ran ahead of everyone. Every few steps, he stopped to fire his gun and reload it, then he ran again.

They had now reentered a wooded area, and it was hard to see where the bullets were coming from. It seemed as if the enemy had increased in size. Each time the smoke cleared, they were bombarded from all sides. It was hard to know where to aim their guns. After a while, the men crouched behind a bush or a tree and would not move.

The lieutenant cursed at them again, but this time it did no good.

"Come on, you idiots!" he screamed. "We'll all get killed if we stay here. We have to move. We have to go across that field."

"That field?" Henry asked in disbelief, pointing with his arm.

It would be impossible to get across.

The field was surrounded by enemy lines. They would be in danger on all sides if they tried to cross.

"Yes, that field," the lieutenant said. He walked up to Henry, grabbed him by the shoulders and pushed him forward.

"Come on!" he shouted at him.

"Come on, yourself," Henry said.

They stared at each other furiously. For a moment, it looked as if they would come to blows.

"Come on, yourself," Henry said again. This time, he said it calmly, like a challenge.

Both of them ran forward. Wilson followed two steps behind them, and, after a while, a few more men followed.

"Come on! Come on!" they shouted.

Suddenly, the soldier who carried the flag gave a loud cry. Waving the flag high in the air, he ran ahead of the others into the open field.

After a moment's hesitation, the regiment surged forward like a huge

wave. Immediately, they were surrounded by gunfire and scattered through the field. Compared to the size of the enemy, they looked like a small handful of men.

Henry ran like a madman. On the other side, there was forest again. If he could make it across, he could take cover behind a tree.

As he ran, he kept his eyes on the flag. It waved gently yet majestically in the wind, and seemed like the most beautiful, the most splendid thing Henry had ever seen. He felt a sudden, desperate love for it. He would give his life for it, he thought. He would give his life, so it could always ride high. He would never let the enemy trample it in the dirt. Never!

Just as he was having these thoughts the sergeant who was carrying the flag, was shot and fell to the ground. Henry rushed to his side and took hold of the flag. The sergeant had died with his hand clasped tightly around the pole. As Henry tried to pull it free, the dead

man's arm swung back and forth, as though he were still alive and did not want to let go.

Wilson saw Henry struggling to pry the flagpole loose and came to his aid. Together, they were able to free the flag from the dead man's grasp. They took hold of the pole, raised the flag high, and ran toward the woods in the forefront of the troops.

Chapter 10
Carrying the Flag

Wilson and Henry had advanced more than halfway across the field. Holding the flag high over their heads, they turned around and looked at the troops fighting behind them. The men were still facing the enemy and firing their rifles, but they were beginning to retreat. They were taking backward steps each time they stopped to reload. The officers were galloping around them, urging them to go forward.

"Where do you think you're going!" they hollered. "Onward! Onward! Shoot into the enemy!"

The regiment had lost ground. At the urging of the officers, some of the men were beginning to move ahead again, but they looked worn out and discouraged.

They moved with their heads down, as though by bowing their heads they could dodge enemy bullets. They seemed to be furious, but their anger was not directed at the enemy. They were angry at their own officers who were screaming at them to go forward.

The officer who was screaming the loudest was the same officer who had described the regiment as a bunch of "mule drivers." Showing great courage, he was belting out orders with his back to the enemy and his face to the troops. Still, Henry could not forgive him for what he had said. He had taken the insult personally. No one was going to call Henry Fleming a mule driver and get away with it.

He had hoped that the regiment—the mule drivers—would prove the officer wrong. He had hoped that the troops would cross the field bravely. It would have been the best revenge. The regiment would have won gloriously, and Henry could have marched up to the officer and said: "So we're mule drivers, are we?"

Now, seeing the number of men who were continuing to retreat, Henry felt ashamed. He hated the enemy for causing him to feel such shame, but he hated his commanding officer even more. He hated him for having so little confidence in his own regiment.

Nevertheless, Henry had to put his hatred aside. He had to rise above his insulted pride and fight for his comrades.

"Give me the flag!" he said to Wilson. "Let me have it!"

Wilson would not let go. They scuffled over the flag, and Henry pushed Wilson to the ground. It was a critical moment,

Henry thought. He had to take charge. He had to give courage and hope to his comrades. If it meant risking his life, he was ready to do it.

He held the flag up high and joined his lieutenant. Together, they howled at the troops to fight on.

It was hard to persuade the men to fight in order to save their reputation and honor, however. All they were beginning to care about was how to save their own skin.

In the thick smoke from gunfire and exploding cannonballs, it was hard to keep a forward direction, or know where to aim one's rifle. Sometimes, the men hit their own comrades by mistake. Sometimes, thinking that they were moving toward enemy fire, they marched toward the rear. Whenever the clouds of smoke cleared, the enemy looked to be thousands strong. Their formations looked like solid walls.

Henry's eardrums were buzzing from

the deafening roar of the battle. Looking around, he became dazed. Here and there, the troops were managing to move forward. For the greater part, however, they were fleeing in panic.

Henry stood amidst the fighting men and held the flag high. It was utter chaos—pandemonium on the battlefield. Enemy bullets whizzed by with even regularity, as though they were being fired by a single machine and not an army of men. Henry tried to keep himself calm, but he was breathing fast.

Wilson walked up to him. "So, I guess it's good-bye," Wilson said. "We're going to die."

"Oh, keep it to yourself, you fool!" Henry replied.

The two friends would not look at each other.

The officers were continuing to shout orders, but the men were crouching down or crawling, trying to find some small hollow on the ground in which to take cover.

The lieutenant stood with his legs apart, and held his sword with the tip on the ground as though it were a cane. His mouth gaped open, but nothing came out of it. He looked like a small child who has just had a crying fit and has no more strength to cry. His lower lip quivered slightly, as though he were talking to himself.

Whenever there was a lull in the fighting and the smoke cleared, the men looked around, anxiously, to see how bad their losses were.

"They're coming at us!" the lieutenant shouted. "My God, they're coming at us!"

The enemy was moving into the field. They were on the attack and closing in fast. They were so close that Henry could see their faces. He was amazed to see that their uniforms seemed brand-new. The gray cloth seemed to glow in the sun. It was as though these rebel uniforms were made out of shining steel.

Before Henry had time to take it all in, the two armies came at each other head on. It was like fighting in hand-to-hand combat. Fire was exchanged rapidly back and forth, and the air became thick with black smoke again. The troops in Henry's regiment were surrounded—trapped. Unless they fought back, they would be slaughtered like animals trapped in a pen.

Henry strained his eyes to see through the smoke, but he could not see anything. After a while, he seated himself on the ground and planted the flag between his knees. By the sound of it, the enemy was losing ground. Fewer and fewer bullets ripped through the air.

The men of his regiment held their fire, and the smoke started to lift. It floated toward the sky like a thin

cloud. Now that it was possible to see, the troops stood still and gazed around them, astonished. The enemy had retreated. The field was empty except for countless dead men.

After a moment of disbelief, the men jumped up and down. They shouted with triumph. They laughed out loud and cheered. They hugged each other and wept with joy.

They were not cowards, after all! They had won! They were heroes!

Chapter 11
Heroes

In other parts of the battlefield, fighting was still going on, but the roar of battle reached Henry's regiment like distant thunder. In the field where they were left standing, there was silence. They were no longer being shot at. They were free to overtake the field.

There were not many soldiers left. The few who had survived gathered in a group and marched ahead to complete their mission. Despite the quiet, however, the survivors were experiencing a new, more disturbing fear: If they were hit by some stray bullet now, their death would be unheroic. It would be the most cruel fate, if they were to be killed now, just as they thought themselves safe and victorious.

The woods they were heading into were filled with soldiers from another regiment of the Union Army. As they drew near, these soldiers cried out from among the trees:

"What took you so long?"

"Where have you been?"

"Had a good time out there?"

The men of the 304th were infuriated by the sarcasm of those remarks. They raised their fists and cursed back. Fistfights would have broken out between the two groups if the lieutenant had not intervened to quiet his men. Henry kept silent but frowned menacingly. The rest of the men lowered their heads and walked on with stooped shoulders,

as though instead of victory, they were carrying the coffin of their honor on their backs.

When they reached the woods, they turned around and looked back over the field. Henry was astonished to discover that it was tiny. The distance they had covered seemed trivial, ridiculous! Also, the time it had taken to complete the charge had been no more than a few minutes. How could such immense fears and such immense courage have occurred in such a small time and space?

With great bitterness, Henry realized that there was a certain truth to the sarcasm of the other soldiers. From their point of view, the charge had been no more than a tempest in a teacup.

Nevertheless, Henry was proud of his performance amidst the danger. He thought over how he had acted and felt a deep satisfaction. He had saved the flag. At certain risk to his life, he had held it up high.

Just as he was congratulating himself on his brave behavior, he saw an officer galloping over to where the troops had gathered. It was the same officer who had called the regiment "mule drivers." He had lost his cap in battle, and his hair was tousled wild by the wind. His face was dark with rage. He seemed to be taking out his fury on his horse. Jerking and pulling savagely at the bridle, he dug his spurs into the poor animal's flanks.

"What a mess you made!" he said to the colonel of the regiment. "What an

awful mess you made! You should have gone after the enemy! You should have routed them. If you had gone after them, you would have demolished them. What a bunch of mud diggers you have for men!"

The colonel stood erect. At first he looked insulted, but then he grew solemn and icily polite.

"We went as far as we could," he said calmly.

"As far as you could?" said the officer. "Did you? Well, that wasn't very far now, was it?" He looked at the colonel with contempt. "Not very far at all, I think. You were supposed to create a diversion, and get the enemy to abandon the attack

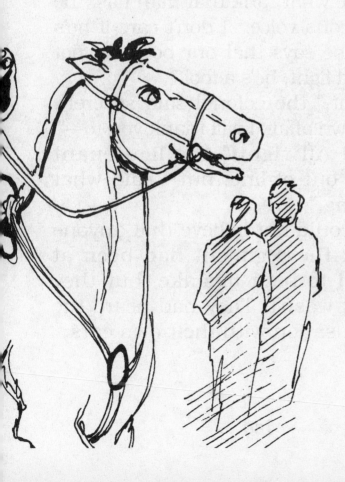

on Waterside. Your ears should tell you how well you succeeded. The battle on Waterside is still raging!"

The colonel listened to the roar of the battle over at Waterside and cursed, lowering his head.

The officer looked at him in silence for a moment, then rode away high and mighty on his horse.

The lieutenant walked up to the colonel.

"I don't care what rank that man has," he said in a furious voice. "I don't care if he's an officer. If he says that our boys did not put up a good fight, he's a fool."

"Lieutenant," the colonel said severely. "This is my own affair. I will thank you to—"

"All right! All right!" the lieutenant said. "I was out of line, but I said what needed saying."

The men could not believe that anyone could think the regiment had been at fault. It had to be a mistake, but they knew that it wasn't. They had heard the officer's accusation with their own ears.

"I wonder what would have satisfied him," Wilson said to Henry. "I've never seen such a man."

"Oh, well," said Henry. "He didn't get what he wanted, and he doesn't care about anything else. We did our best. We fought a good fight."

"I'll say!" Wilson said. "We held our own! But it's no fun, fighting for people who don't appreciate anything you do. No matter what, it's never good enough. I've half a mind to stay put next time around. Let them fight the battle themselves, if they know so much."

"We did the best job we could have done at the time. That's all that matters," Henry said. "Both of us were brave. I'd like to break the neck of anyone who says we weren't."

"I heard a fellow say that the two of us

were the best in the regiment. How about that!"

"A fellow said that?" Henry said. "What fellow?"

Before Wilson could answer, a bunch of men came running over.

"Hey, Fleming!" they said. "Have you heard?"

"Heard what?"

"The colonel called the lieutenant to him and said, 'Who was that lad who carried the flag?' The lieutenant spoke right up. 'That's Fleming,' he said. 'That

boy is a crackerjack!' By God, that's just what he said: Crackerjack. 'He's a very good man to have,' the colonel said. 'He kept the flag way to the front.' 'You bet!' said the lieutenant. 'And there's another fellow, name of Wilson, who was right up there with him. They were at the head of the charge, howling like Indians the whole time.'"

"He said that?" Wilson said.

"You bet he did!"

"Oh, go away. You're lying!" said Henry.

"It's no lie," another man said. "The general said that both of you deserve to be major generals."

"He never said that," said Wilson.

"Oh, go to blazes," said Henry.

Despite their protests, two friends felt pleasure and pride. They exchanged a secret glance of joy between themselves, but among the others they went on pretending that they did not believe a word.

Soon, they forgot all the bad things about the battle. They were happy. Their hearts swelled with joy, and with love and gratitude for their lieutenant and their colonel. How kind they both were! How just and clearsighted! These officers had seen just how heroic Fleming and Wilson really were.

Chapter 12
Sacrifices

When the enemy attacked again, Henry felt calm and self-confident. He marched unafraid, carrying the flag up high. When he saw other men try to dodge and duck away from enemy fire, he felt superior.

As he marched, he watched the battlefield in the valley below. Four different battles were going on at once. Around him, however, only small skirmishes were being fought. The gunfire did not create any smoke to speak of, and Henry could observe the larger battles clearly.

The opposing armies looked like huge waves. They swelled and broke over each other with a tremendous roar. Some times, one army won a particular assault, sometimes the other. After every attack, both sides regrouped their forces, then went at it again. No victory seemed to be decisive. In any case, Henry could not tell which side was which. Both flags looked like identical blotches of red, gleaming like flames amidst the black smoke of gunfire.

When the time came for his regiment to move out of the woods down to the plain, the troops of the 304th were a pitiful sight. They had lost weight, and they had dark circles under their eyes. Their uniforms were tattered, and their hair was dirty and uncombed. They walked with a worn-out gait. Yet, when they joined another regiment and pre-pared to fight together, they pounded cartridges into the barrels of their rifles and fired with fierce, astounding energy.

Henry marched at the forefront of the combined forces, carrying the flag.

He could now see that the enemy line was longer and deeper than he had thought. The enemy soldiers had excited faces and were coming at the troops in a slow, steady run. The men fired at them, no longer waiting to be given the command. They knew what to do by now. They were experienced veterans.

Immediately, the enemy took cover behind the long stone wall of an abandoned farm. Protected by it, they fired back. The men of Henry's regiment were exposed and felt trapped again. They were like open targets for the enemy to shoot at. With bitterness and outrage, they remembered how the officer had called them "mud diggers." Well! They were going to show everyone that they could win this fight!

They did not back off.

Henry felt horrible hatred for the officer who had called him and his comrades "mud diggers." As if mule drivers had not been enough! He wanted to die just to prove the officer wrong. "Yes," he thought. "My dead body will put him to shame. My dead body will be my revenge."

Henry decided that he was not going to budge no matter what happened. He was not going to surrender the flag. He would die first.

He looked around in dismay. His comrades were being killed left and right. The wounded were trying to crawl away to the rear, but most of them could not make it. They just lay on the ground, moaning.

Henry looked around to see how Wilson was doing. Through the thick smoke, he could see a dim figure fighting so fiercely, he looked like a baited bear. That had to be Wilson! Henry observed that the lieutenant, too, was fighting with great courage.

Although the 304th was fighting courageously, it was in danger of surrendering its position. The colonel came running along the back of the line.

"We must charge them!" he shouted. "We must charge them!"

The other officers went among the men, shouting, "Charge! Charge!" There was a nervousness in their voices, as though they were expecting the men to rebel.

Henry calculated the distance between himself and the enemy line. It wasn't too far. Still, he would have to run the distance without cover. There was no other way. It had to be done. The regiment had to push the enemy away from the wall.

He looked back at his comrades. He expected to see hesitant, worn-out faces. To his astonishment, he saw that the men looked fierce—ready and eager to attack. As the lieutenant yelled the command, they sprang forward in leaps. They ran with an extraordinary force. They looked like madmen. Their superhuman energy was like the thrashing crisis that is produced by a fatal fever—the final strength that comes right before death.

Henry kept to the front, ahead of everyone. With one arm, he held up the flag; and with the other, he waved to his comrades to follow.

"Come on! Come on!" he cried.

The thick smoke looked as if it were being gashed by little knives of fire. He could barely see ahead of him, but he knew that behind the smoke lay the wall that was protecting the enemy. He kept urging the men to advance. However, the men did not need to be urged. Even though men were falling left and right, covering the ground between the woods and the fence with their corpses, those who remained upright ran forward toward the enemy front. They were hurling themselves into the line of fire.

Henry shrieked and shouted, so as to

be heard over the screeching bullets and exploding shells: "Come on! Come on!"

Henry was not afraid of death. If he had to, he could make the supreme sacrifice—his life. No bullet was going to stop him from reaching the stone wall. No bullet and no enemy had the power to stop him!

Henry experienced a strange joy. Now

that he was not afraid of death, he was afraid of nothing.

At last, the troops got to the wall and climbed over it. Henry expected that the two armies would now clash. They would come together body to body, arm to arm. But the enemy soldiers had abandoned their positions and were fleeing. The few, isolated bands of men who stood their ground and fought back scattered after only a moment.

Henry thought that it was all over. Then he saw that, to the far right, a small part of the enemy line held up. The rebel soldiers were crouching behind posts and rails. Their flag was waving fiercely over their heads and they were firing their guns, screaming and yelling with rage.

The Union troops went at them, as though they meant to strangle them with their bare hands.

Henry wanted to capture the enemy flag. It was not going to escape from him. Nothing was going to stand in his way. He was going to fight tooth and nail to get it—to lower it in defeat to the ground.

He leapt forward. Ahead of him, four enemy soldiers were on their hands and knees and were quivering as though they had been struck by a bolt from the sky. In the middle of them, also on his knees, was the standard bearer. His body was riddled with bullets, but he

was still struggling to hold up his flag. He strained to get up on his feet, as he hugged the flag to his chest. Looking like a ghost with his bleeding wounds and his pale, ashen face, he stumbled and staggered in an effort to get away.

Henry was too far away to stop him, but Wilson was nearby. He sprang on him like a panther on prey, wrestled the flag from him and raised it triumphantly high in the air. The standard bearer fell to the ground face down, and his body twisted horribly, then lay still in a puddle of blood. The enemy's flag had been captured. The men of the 304th threw their caps into the air and cheered.

The rebel soldiers, who were on their knees, surrendered to the Union troops, who formed a circle and watched the captured men with curiosity. One of the prisoners, who had a superficial wound on his foot, was cursing the men.

"You can go to the devil," he said with bitter rage. "You are a plague on this land."

Apparently, he did not know how prisoners should behave.

Another prisoner, who looked to be no more than a boy, was quite calm. He chatted with the men about the war, the different battles he had been in, the condition of his army. He was good-natured and friendly.

A third prisoner was silent and sullen. The Union men could not get a word out of him.

Another man looked deeply humiliated and worried. Henry guessed that he was thinking of what might be awaiting him: a dark dungeon, starvation, beatings. He seemed to be dreading his prisoner's fate.

Soon, the Union men lost interest in the prisoners. They sat down on the ground with their backs against a fence and rested. Now and then, they took a shot at a fleeing enemy soldier who lagged behind the retreating rebels.

The fighting was over.

Wilson walked about, carrying the

enemy flag like a trophy. Henry lay down on the grass. After a while, Wilson joined him, and the two friends lay side by side. They were exhausted, but happy.

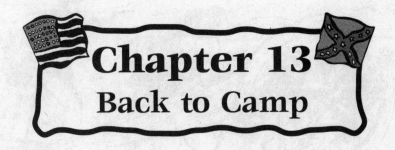

Chapter 13
Back to Camp

The constant roaring of battle was beginning to lessen. It sounded weaker and weaker. Now and then, the sound of cannon fire could be heard in the far distance, but the sound of gunfire had all but ceased. Henry and Wilson had become so used to constant loud noise that the silence was making them feel uneasy. Fighting had become a way of life. What were they supposed to do with themselves now?

They looked over at the camp. Small companies were being ordered to march this way and that. The artillery battery was leisurely wheeling cannons to a new position.

Henry got up.

"Well, what now?" he said. He shaded his eyes with his hand and looked back over the field they had just captured. "I bet you we're going to march back through the field, and cross the river again," he told Wilson.

"Well, I swear!" said Wilson. "That means we'll be going back where we started from."

"You'll see," said Henry.

Sure enough, the regiment was given orders to march back.

The men stretched their arms over their heads and tried to shake the stiffness out of their legs. From the looks on their faces and the groans of protest they made, they seemed to mind marching back to safety as much as they had minded going into battle. They were worn out.

The troops marched down to the plain, where they were joined by the other regiment of their brigade. They formed a single column and marched in formation until they entered the woods. Then they split up into small unruly groups and went trudging on among the trees, dragging their feet. They were a sorry sight. With their faces coated with sweat and soot, their clothes dusty and tattered, they looked like a bunch of bandits. At last, they reached the river.

"Well," Henry said to Wilson. "It's finally over."

"By God, it is," said Wilson.

The troops crossed the river and marched toward camp.

It took a long time for Henry to relax. It was hard to believe that the fighting was really over. He had lived under a constant danger of being shot for so long, it had seemed like forever. Yet he had withstood it all. He had come out alive.

Henry looked back on all that had happened, and felt great satisfaction. He had a lot to be proud of. Everything that he had done in the presence of his comrades had been admirable. In terms of what his comrades had seen, he was nothing but a hero. They had praised his heroism. They looked up to him, and with good reason.

Nevertheless, there was that part of his behavior that no one knew about.

There was the time he had run for his life. He blushed when he remembered it.

"What's the matter, Henry?" Wilson asked his friend.

Henry kicked a rock in his path and cursed. He pretended that he was irritated at the roughness of the ground, which made walking hard. If you did not look out, you could stumble and fall on your face.

He walked with his head down. His cowardice and his lies about it filled him with a terrible shame.

His cowardice and lying were not the only things he felt bad about. There was the tattered man, who had been so kind. Though badly wounded himself, he had kept worrying about Henry's invented wounds. Then there was Jim Conklin. How bravely he had died!

Henry turned pale and broke into a cold sweat as it all came back to his mind. As much as he tried to think about his bravery, the memory of his earlier cowardice made him feel an agony of shame. What if someone were watching him closely at that moment? What if someone could read the shame on his face and guess at the truth?

Henry tried to walk at some distance from his comrades, so they could not get too close a look at his face. The men seemed deep in their own thoughts, though; no one seemed to be concerned about Henry.

"I know that we won," one of the men said. "But if you asked me, I'd say we got a beating. Look at us!"

"A beating! You must be kidding," said another. "We whipped the enemy thoroughly. We came in right behind them and whipped them."

"Oh, hush about all this coming in behind them. Who came in behind them? They came in behind us!"

The argument went back and forth. After a while, Henry felt safe to have his shameful thoughts. The thing that was impossible to live down was how he had treated the tattered man. He had not thanked him for his kindness, let alone return it. He had abandoned him to wander off helplessly in a corpse-filled field. Then, when he got back to camp, instead of hanging his head down and keeping silent, he had had the nerve to boast. Oh, how shameful those fake boasts had been! Oh, how he despised himself for making them!

The world suddenly seemed a beautiful, gentle place. The rain fell softly on his skin, as if it meant to caress him. The river flowed quietly, gleaming like silver. Henry looked up, to see a golden ray of sun gliding between two black clouds.

Sooner or later, the sky would clear and the sun would shine.

The End

ABOUT THE AUTHOR

STEPHEN CRANE was born in Newark, New Jersey, on November 1, 1871. The youngest of 14 children, Crane attended only one semester of college before moving to New York to become a professional writer.

The Red Badge of Courage was first published in 1895. The novel earned Crane great success and international acclaim at the age of 24. Other works by Crane include his famous short story "The Open Boat." Crane died of tuberculosis in 1900, when he was just 28 years old.

The Young Collector's
Illustrated Classics

The Adventures of Huckleberry Finn
The Adventures of Robin Hood
The Adventures of Sherlock Holmes
The Adventures of Tom Sawyer
Anne of Green Gables
Black Beauty
Call of the Wild
Dracula
Frankenstein
Gulliver's Travels
Heidi
The Hunchback of Notre Dame
A Little Princess
Little Women
Moby Dick
Oliver Twist
Peter Pan
The Prince and the Pauper
Rebecca of Sunnybrook Farm
The Red Badge of Courage
The Secret Garden
The Strange Case of Dr. Jekyll and Mr. Hyde
Swiss Family Robinson
Tales of Terror and Suspense
The Time Machine
Treasure Island
20,000 Leagues Under the Sea
White Fang

These Illustrated Classics are available for special
and educational sales from:
www.kidsbooks.com

Kidsbooks, Inc.
3535 West Peterson Avenue
Chicago, IL 60659
(800) 515-5437